J Enderl
Enderle, Dotti, 1954- author.
Plop! /

34028083968678
FM $27.07   ocn852681922
02/27/14

W9-DDK-285

3 4028 08396 8678
HARRIS COUNTY PUBLIC LIBRARY

DISCARDS

DISCARDS

GHOST DETECTORS

Plop!

BOOK 14

BY
DOTTI ENDERLE

ILLUSTRATED BY
HOWARD MCWILLIAM

magic
wagon

visit us at www.abdopublishing.com

Published by Magic Wagon, a division of the ABDO Group, PO Box 398166, Edina, MN 55439. Copyright © 2014 by Abdo Consulting Group, Inc. International copyrights reserved in all countries. All rights reserved. No part of this book may be reproduced in any form without written permission from the publisher.

Calico Chapter Books™ is a trademark and logo of Magic Wagon.

Printed in the United States of America, North Mankato, MN.
102013
012014

 This book contains at least 10% recycled materials.

Text by Dotti Enderle
Illustrations by Howard McWilliam
Edited by Stephanie Hedlund and Rochelle Baltzer
Cover and interior design by Jaime Martens

Library of Congress Cataloging-in-Publication Data

Enderle, Dotti, 1954- author.
  Plop! / by Dotti Enderle ; illustrated by Howard McWilliam.
    pages cm. -- (Ghost detectors ; book 14)
  Summary: When Grandma Eunice gives Malcolm a strange bottle that she "won" during the 1939 World's Fair, it turns out to contain the ectoplasm of the performer that she tricked--so if Malcolm wants to keep his bottle he is going to have to figure out how to evict this stubborn ghost.
  ISBN 978-1-62402-002-5
1. Ghost stories. 2. Grandmothers--Juvenile fiction. 3. New York World's Fair (1939-1940 : New York, N.Y.)--Juvenile fiction. 4. Humorous stories. [1. Ghosts--Fiction. 2. Grandmothers--Fiction. 3. New York World's Fair (1939-1940 : New York, N.Y.)--Fiction. 4. Humorous stories.] I. McWilliam, Howard, 1977- illustrator. II. Title. III. Series: Enderle, Dotti, 1954- Ghost Detectors ; bk. 14.
  PZ7.E69645Pm 2014
  813.6--dc23   2013025333

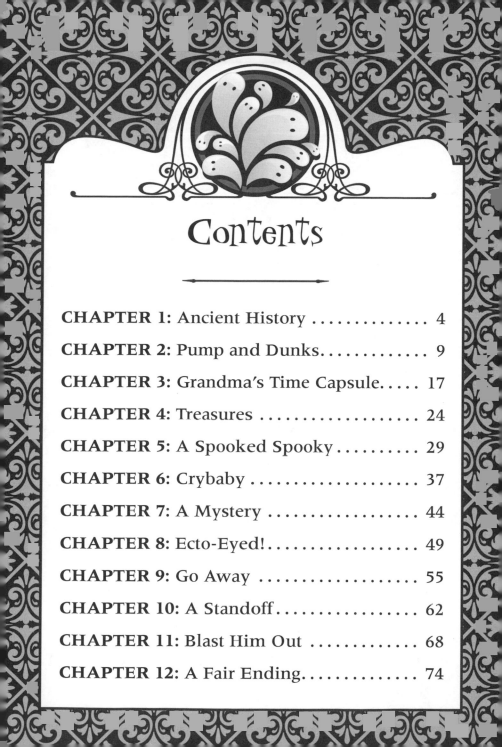

Contents

Ancient History

"**N**OOOOOOO!"

Malcolm plugged his fingers in his ears. If his sister, Cocoa, screamed one more time, it'd shatter his eardrums. He just wanted to eat his dinner in peace— even though it was liver and onions. *Bleh.*

"Calm down," Malcolm's mom said. "It's not a big deal."

As usual, his dad was pretending to read the newspaper. He always avoided dinner drama.

Cocoa's eyes bloomed wide, putting even more smudgy cracks in her carrot-orange eye shadow. "It *is* a big deal! I promised my friends I'd go with them to the movies. It's the opening weekend of *Whispers of Love*. I can't miss it!"

"Let her go," Malcolm said. "Maybe it'll teach her how to whisper."

Cocoa glared. "Shut it, dork. This isn't about you."

"It's about all of us," Malcolm's mom insisted. She looked at his dad. "Right?"

"Um-huh," he said, turning to the sports page.

As much as Malcolm hated to admit, he agreed with Cocoa on this one. Instead of spending a Saturday lying around, reading *Bizarr-O* magazine or chasing ghosts, he had to spend it helping clean out an old house.

"Don't forget," his mom said, "this was the house where Grandma Eunice grew up. It has a history."

Malcolm looked at his great-grandma. He didn't know how old she was, but she still tried to crank the telephone to call someone. The house had a history all right—ancient history!

Grandma Eunice was poking peas in her mashed potatoes to make a smiley face. "I can't believe they're tearing down that old house. That's where I learned to tie my shoes. To ride a bike. And I kissed Earl Grimsby under that porch."

"Ewwww!!!" Cocoa wailed.

Grandma tossed one of the peas in the air and caught it in her mouth. "What? Earl was a hottie."

Cocoa gagged, causing foamy spit to glisten on her Mango Tango lip gloss.

Even Malcolm's dad grimaced behind his newspaper.

His mom put her foot down. "Cocoa, you can go to the movies after we clean out the house. None of you have ever been to Grandma's childhood home. It's the only time you'll get to see it before it's torn down. We need to make sure that nothing valuable is left behind."

Malcolm couldn't imagine what could be so valuable in an old house that no one's lived in for over fifty years. But it would be kind of cool to see where Grandma Eunice lived when she was a kid.

"Can I bring Dandy?" Malcolm asked. If he had to give up a Saturday, he could at least have his best friend along to make it more fun.

"Dandy's always welcome," his mom answered.

Great! Who knew what kind of crazy stuff they might dig up there. It could be an adventure.

Pump and Dunks

Malcolm and Dandy both gazed up as the car pulled into the gravel driveway.

"Someone actually lived here?" Dandy whispered.

"I'm sure it looked better a million years ago when Grandma Eunice was a kid," Malcolm whispered back.

Malcolm had a hard time imagining this place bright and new. It was a large two-

story with broken shutters and sagging window boxes. The large front porch stuck out like a swollen tongue.

"Yay!" Grandma said as they helped her out of the car. "It looks better than I expected."

Malcolm and Dandy exchanged a look. Better?

"Hey, diddle, diddle," Grandma sang, "can you solve this riddle?"

"We don't have time for riddles," Malcolm's mom said. "We need to get busy."

Cocoa flicked away a gnat with her diamond-sparkled fingernail. "The riddle is how do we clean out this house without the ceiling falling on us?"

"Don't worry," Malcolm said. "Nothing can crack your bowling-ball head."

She waved her fist in his face. "But I can crack yours."

He patted his mouth, faking a yawn.

"Careful," Malcolm's mom said as she walked up the porch steps. "It's rickety."

They all followed, including Grandma Eunice. She turned back to Malcolm and Dandy. "Here's the riddle."

They listened closely.

"How am I going to get up on the porch?" Grandma Eunice asked.

That was a tough riddle since there was no wheelchair ramp.

"I give up," Malcolm said.

Grandma Eunice hopped out of her wheelchair and vaulted onto the porch. "Would you hand me that, please?"

Malcolm and Dandy picked up the wheelchair and set it on the porch.

"Do you even need this wheelchair?" Malcolm asked.

"I need it more than you do. I've told you before—your mother thinks I'm one banana short of a bunch, so I'm playing along," she said with a wink. Then she sat down and rolled into the house.

Dandy shook his head. "Your grandma's a real oddball."

Malcolm grinned. "You just noticed?"

As they raced up the steps—"Yeow!"— Dandy's foot crashed through, making a hole that swallowed his leg all the way to his knee.

He tugged it a few times. "I'm stuck!"

"Can you twist your leg to the side and lift it up?" Malcolm asked.

Dandy twisted. "Nope."

"Can you wiggle your foot? Maybe that will loosen the board."

Dandy wiggled. "Nope."

"Can you dance around a little? That should work."

Dandy danced. It didn't work.

"Okay," Malcolm said. "I've got an idea. I'm going to go underneath and shove your foot up. You pull at the same time."

Dandy nodded. "Just hurry! My toes are falling asleep."

Malcolm went to the side of the porch, squatted down, and spread back the tall weeds that were growing around it. It was dark and damp, and it smelled a lot like wet socks. But he got on his hands and knees and slinked under.

It was kind of creepy down there. And even creepier knowing that this was where Grandma Eunice had kissed some boy named Earl. Yuck!

Malcolm finally got to the steps and crab-crawled underneath. "Here's the problem!" he called up. "Your shoe is caught on a board."

"Can you get it loose?" Dandy asked.

"I'm going to push. You pull."

"Okay. But these are my brand-new Pump and Dunk sneakers. If I get them scuffed up, my dad will kill me."

"Don't worry," Malcolm said. "Ready?" Malcolm grabbed Dandy's foot and shoved. "Pull!"

Dandy tugged, yanked, and strained.

Malcolm thrust and shoved and—"Whoa!"—Dandy's foot popped loose. Malcolm ducked away to keep from getting kicked in the chin.

Dandy's leg went up and out as he plopped on the ground.

Malcolm poked his head through the hole like a jack-in-the-box. "Are you okay?"

Dandy had that pinched look on his face like he'd swallowed icky medicine. Then Malcolm saw why. Right across the front of his fancy Pump and Dunks was a black scuff the size of a garden snake.

"Dude, your dad is going to kill you," Malcolm said.

Dandy licked his thumb and tried wiping off the mark. "But on the bright side, my toes are awake."

"Malcolm!" Cocoa bellowed. "Stop playing around and come help!"

Malcolm crab-crawled back out. "Let's go." He and Dandy hurdled onto the porch just like Grandma Eunice, then hurried inside.

Grandma's Time Capsule

Malcolm didn't think the inside of the house could look as bad as the front. But he also didn't think he'd get a C on his math test last week. There were leaning doors, a tilted staircase, and a checkered rug. It was like being in a fun house.

"This place is really old," Dandy said as they walked down the hall.

"I know. Grandma Eunice should've sold it a long time ago."

Dandy pointed to some cobwebs in the corner. "You think there are ghosts here?"

Malcolm shook his head. "Nah. Grandma would've scared them all off."

They went into Grandma Eunice's old bedroom. She was by the bed, peeking under the mattress. Malcolm bent over and peeked in, too.

"What are you looking for?"

"I used to hide things here," she said. "This is where I hid my diary and my movie star magazines. I even hid my bad report cards."

Malcolm lifted the mattress a little higher. "All I see are peanut hulls."

She snapped her fingers. "That's why the mattress was so lumpy!"

"It doesn't look like anything is hidden here."

"Maybe not." Then she rolled her wheelchair to the bedroom window. "But there is something hidden out there."

Malcolm and Dandy both peered out.

"Back in 1939," she said, "I buried a time capsule."

Dandy's face lit up. "A time capsule? Like at NASA?"

Malcolm rolled his eyes. "No, silly, that's a space capsule."

Grandma clacked her dentures. "I tried launching it into space, but my slingshot wasn't strong enough."

Malcolm smiled, thinking about her with a slingshot. "Do you want us to dig it up?"

"Yep." She winked at him. "There's a lot of great stuff inside."

Great stuff? He couldn't wait! "Where did you bury it?"

She pointed to the corner of the rickety fence. "See that rose bush?"

Malcolm and Dandy leaned closer to the window. "Yeah," Malcolm said.

"I didn't bury it there. Those thorns are too darn prickly."

"Then where did you bury it?"

She pointed to the other side of the yard. "In that corner by the petunias."

Malcolm gazed over at the little inky flowers. "Okay." He nudged Dandy. "Come on!"

They rushed out to the toolshed. There was only one shovel, so Malcolm did the digging.

"How deep do you think it is?" Dandy asked.

"Probably not too deep," Malcolm answered. "Grandma was just a little girl. She probably didn't have the strength to dig far."

But five minutes later, Malcolm was still shoveling.

"Boy, your grandma sure was strong," Dandy said.

Malcolm exhaled and wiped some sweat from his forehead. "I guess she didn't want any dogs digging it up."

He thought, *Maybe she didn't want* anyone *digging it up!*

Just when he was about to give up, the shovel pinged something that sounded like tin. "There it is!" He dropped down on his knees and tugged out a rusty old mailbox.

Dandy's eyes bulged. "Wow! They had mail back in 1939?"

"Of course," Malcolm said. "How do you think they sent letters?"

"The same way everyone does. On the computer."

"Nope. They only had snail mail back then."

Malcolm wanted to open it right then, but it didn't seem fair. "Let's take it back to Grandma," he suggested.

"Uh, Malcolm . . . don't you think you should fill in the hole first?"

Malcolm shrugged. "Let's fill it in later."

Dandy pointed down. "Let's fill it in now."

Neither of the boys had noticed that while Malcolm was digging, he'd flung a heap of dirt on Dandy's feet . . . all the way up to his knees!

Malcolm set the mailbox down and quickly freed Dandy. They both stared at his dirt-filled Pump and Dunks.

Dandy sighed. "My dad's going to kill me."

Treasures

"**W**e've got it!" Malcolm called as they raced back inside.

Grandma clapped her hands. "Yay! There is a lot of fun stuff in here."

"Like video games?" Dandy asked, eyes bright.

Grandma Eunice beamed. "Like postcards."

Postcards? Malcolm thought. *It really is a mailbox.*

"Everyone gather 'round!" Grandma called. She hugged the dirty old mailbox close while Malcolm's mom and Cocoa joined them.

"Gross," Cocoa said, stepping back. "What's in that nasty old can?"

Mom raised an eyebrow and smiled. "Love letters from Earl?"

"Oh, no," Grandma said. "Earl and I met when we were fifteen." She made kissy sounds.

"Ew," Cocoa said, her black eyeliner crinkling. "Can we not talk about

Grandma's love life?"

Malcolm was bouncing from foot to foot. "Come on, let's see what's in there."

Grandma held the front of the mailbox out toward him. "Pull."

He grabbed the handle and yanked. The door slowly creaked open.

"Wow," Dandy said. It was stuffed full.

Grandma reached in. "Now let's have a look." She shuffled some things around. "Oh, look! It's my *Gone with the Wind* snow globe." She took it out and shook it. Soft white flakes flurried about.

Mom took the snow globe and set it aside. "That's wonderful!"

Grandma reached in again. "Oh, Cocoa, you'll want this." She brought out a small blue cup with a picture of a dimpled girl with ringlets.

Cocoa curled her lip. "Uh, why would I want that?"

"It's a Shirley Temple mug," Grandma said. "I got it when I went to see one of her movies."

"I bet it's a collector's item, Cocoa," Mom told her. "It's probably worth some money."

Cocoa snatched it at warp speed. "Thanks, Grandma."

Malcolm gave Cocoa a shove. "Ditz."

She shoved back. "Dork."

Grandma Eunice fluttered her hand and clacked her dentures. "Oh, I'd completely forgotten! That's the year I went to the World's Fair."

She took out a tall, skinny bottle that was the color of caramel ice cream. The neck spiraled like a snake, and the top

was closed tight with a heavy cork. On the side were the words, *1939 World's Fair. The World of Tomorrow.*

"Would you like it?" she asked Malcolm.

Malcolm took it. "Awesome! Thanks, Grandma." Unlike Cocoa, he meant it. He'd never seen a bottle this cool.

Grandma dug around some more, finding a pair of *Wizard of Oz* ruby slipper socks, a book called *Thimble Summer*, and a small vinyl record of a song called "Jeepers Creepers." But Malcolm kept staring at the bottle.

"What do you think is in there?" Dandy whispered.

Malcolm shook his head. "I don't know. But as soon as we get back to my house, we'll uncork it and find out."

A Spooked Spooky

Malcolm was happy to be home because a) he was tired from moving boxes of Grandma Eunice's stuff, b) he didn't have to listen to his sister whine anymore, and c) he was dying to get this bottle open to see what was inside.

He grabbed a corkscrew from the kitchen. "Come on," he told Dandy. They hurried down into Malcolm's basement lab.

Dandy turned on Malcolm's Ecto-Handheld-Automatic-Heat-Sensitive-Laser-Enhanced Specter Detector so that Malcolm's ghostly dog, Spooky, could play. The pooch appeared like magic, bounding and frisky. *Yip! Yip!*

"Good boy," Dandy said. But just as he said it, Spooky turned, sniffed, then growled up at the bottle in Malcolm's hand.

Malcolm had already started twisting the corkscrew into the cork. He stopped once Spooky went into a frenzy.

Grrrrr!

"What do you think's wrong with him?" Dandy asked.

Malcolm twitched his mouth, thinking. He looked down at Spooky, then at the bottle, then back at Spooky. "Hmmm..."

He bent down and put the bottle close to the snarling mutt.

Spooky went into hyper-mode. *Grrrrr! Ruff! Ruff!* Malcolm hadn't seen him this riled up since the silly pooch had gotten spooked over a mummy's curse.

"Wow," Malcolm said. "Now I really want to know what's in here." He started turning the corkscrew even faster.

Dandy gulped like he'd just swallowed a quarter. "Maybe we shouldn't open it. If Spooky doesn't like it, then we probably won't either."

Malcolm continued drilling into the cork. "Don't be silly. He probably just senses some weird vibes from a long time ago."

"Weird vibes?"

"You know, like if someone was holding it while they cheated at the balloon pop booth. Or the ring toss."

Dandy scratched his head. "Would your grandmother do something like that?"

Malcolm smiled. "Have you met her?"

Dandy nodded. "Oh, right."

Spooky continued to hop and spit and growl.

Malcolm nodded toward the ghost detector. "Better turn that off before Spooky flips himself into a pretzel."

"Yeah," Dandy agreed. "It'd take forever for him to untwist." He clicked off the detector, and Spooky vanished into thin air.

Once Malcolm had the corkscrew in tight, he pulled and tugged and yanked and *Pop*! "Ha ha! It's open!"

"Quick," Dandy said. "Let's see what's inside."

Malcolm turned the bottle upside down and shook it. But a whole lot of nothing came out.

Just like Spooky, Malcolm went, "Grrrrr!" He shook the bottle again. "I know there's something in there!"

"Why don't you shine a flashlight in it?" Dandy suggested.

"Because the neck is all twisty. It wouldn't work."

"Yeah," Dandy said. "It looks like the waterslide at Splash Around Park."

Malcolm snapped his fingers. "I've got an idea."

If there was one thing Malcolm was good at, it was ideas. He dug through his box of gadgets, and took out a roll of tape and some wire.

Dandy watched, wide-eyed. "What are you going to do with that?"

"I'm going to snag it."

Malcolm wound the tape around the end of the wire so that the sticky part was facing out. Then he carefully inserted it into the bottle. It wasn't easy going through the bottle's spiral neck, but finally, he got it down the neck.

"Hurry," Dandy said. "The suspense is killing me."

Malcolm knew exactly what he meant. It was killing him too. He took a deep breath, twirled the wire around, then brought it back up.

Both boys moved close, not wanting to miss the grand entrance of whatever was on the end of that tape. Malcolm finally pulled it out and . . .

"Ew," Dandy said. "Just some green mildew."

Malcolm slumped. "I still have a feeling there's something in there."

Dandy nodded. "I guess it doesn't want to get snagged."

Malcolm sighed. "Oh well."

"You should be happy," Dandy said. "If it got Spooky all in a tizzy, then maybe it should stay in the bottle."

"Maybe you're right," Malcolm said. But that was what bothered him most. If there was nothing in there, then why did it rate so high on Spooky's radar?

Crybaby

At bedtime, Malcolm put the bottle on the bookcase over his bed. Then he yawned, stretched, curled up, and—*zzzzzz*—went to sleep.

He hadn't been dozing long, when—*plop!*—something dripped on his head. He stirred a little and wiped it away.

Then—*plop!*—it happened again. This time he blinked, wiped it off, and went back to sleep.

Then came a third *plop!*

Malcolm sat straight up. "What is that?" He wiped at something gooey on his forehead. He turned on the lamp and . . . Yikes! It was green, glowing, and pulsating. Like Cocoa's tongue after she ate a lime Popsicle.

"Gah!" Malcolm looked up at the bookcase. The World's Fair bottle was lying on its side. Big globs of green gunk were plopping all over his pillow. He grabbed the bottle and set it upright.

What is this stuff? he wondered.

He carefully picked up the bottle, brought it to his nose, and sniffed. *Bleh.* It smelled like old pennies. He took it to the bathroom sink and turned it upside down. A slow moment later—*plop!*— another drop fell.

He touched it with his finger. Hmmm . . . warm and slimy. It was just as he suspected.

"Ectoplasm," he said out loud. And where there's ectoplasm, there's a ghost. "I knew there was something inside."

Malcolm pushed in the cork, sealing the bottle shut. But when he woke up the next morning—*plop! plop! plop!*—the bottle was open and dripping ecto all over his face.

Malcolm found Grandma Eunice at the kitchen table, eating purple pancakes.

"Grandma, your pancakes look like wimpy turnips."

Grandma poured on some syrup. "Well, you know what I always say. There just isn't enough purple food."

She never said that, but he didn't argue.

She stabbed a big chunk with her fork and held it out to Malcolm. "Would you like some?"

He stepped back. "No, I'm good."

She shrugged, then crammed it into her mouth.

"Uh, why are your pancakes purple?" he asked.

Grandma swallowed the big hunk. "Prune juice," she answered. "Are you sure you don't want some?"

"Positive." Malcolm held up the World's Fair bottle. He'd replaced the cork again. "Grandma, how did you get this? Did you buy it? Win it? Was it a giveaway?"

Grandma wiped some syrup from her chin. "I won it, of course. There was a

man who said he could guess my exact weight."

"Did he guess?"

She twirled a bit of pancake in the syrup. "He said I weighed ninety-eight pounds."

"Was he wrong?"

"Nope. That's exactly how much I weighed."

"Then how did you trick him?"

She raised an eyebrow. "I rolled a watermelon onto the scales with me."

"Grandma, that's cheating!"

"Yeah," she said, jabbing more pancake with her fork. "I was going to confess, but he started pitching a fit. Stomping up and down. He turned into a real crybaby."

"A crybaby?"

Grandma talked and chewed at the same time. "Yep. Just like Cocoa when I ask her to put ointment on my feet."

Malcolm knew Cocoa was a crybaby, but putting ointment on Grandma's scaly old feet was something to cry about. "What did he say?"

Grandma pretended to whine. "He said, 'Ruined! Ruined! I will never guess weights again!' He shoved the bottle at me and groaned, 'I just want to crawl into this bottle and hide forever!'"

"Uh, what happened next?"

Grandma shrugged. "I drank the root beer that was inside the bottle and took it home."

"And nothing strange happened with the bottle after that?"

"Nope. I took it out the next day and buried it in my time capsule. I was really disappointed. I wanted to win a Kewpie doll instead. So when you think about it, he tricked *me*."

Malcolm didn't know what a Kewpie doll was, but they probably weren't haunted. "Okay. Thanks, Grandma."

"Anytime," she said, mushing more purple pancake into her mouth.

Malcolm rushed to the phone. "Dandy, get over here now."

A Mystery

"I would've been here sooner," Dandy said, "but I had to wait till my dad decided if he was going to ground me. He was really mad about my Pump and Dunks. But he said I had to do the dishes for a week instead."

"I feel bad about that," Malcolm told him. "It was all my fault."

Dandy waved it off. "Don't worry. Mom does all the cooking. And since she's

going to be out of town this week, Dad will want to eat out." He nodded toward the bottle. "Did you find out what was in there?"

"Almost," Malcolm said. He explained what had happened.

"So what are you going to do?" Dandy wondered. "Bury it again?"

Malcolm shook his head. "Nope. I'm going to figure out who's in there and how to get him out."

"Whoa, Malcolm, that could be dangerous."

Malcolm raised an eyebrow. "Danger is my middle name."

"I thought your middle name was Sherman."

"I changed it," Malcolm said.

"Danger is an awesome name." Dandy scratched his head. "So how are we going to find out who's haunting this bottle?"

Malcolm grabbed his laptop. "We'll do some research." He typed in *World's Fair, 1939, collector bottle*. Up popped a picture of a white vinegar bottle that looked like a baseball with a spout. On the side was written, *World's Fair 1939*.

"That's not the same one," Dandy pointed out.

Malcolm searched again. That white bottle was the only one that showed up. "There's not one like this one on the Internet. Looks like this is one of a kind."

"I bet it's worth a jillion dollars," Dandy said.

Malcolm shook his head. "Not with a ghost in it."

He typed in the keywords again, but this time he added *guess your weight*. The first thing to come up was an article dated May 17, 1939. The headline: *Weight Guesser Outguessed*.

Malcolm read the article out loud.

"Pervious Peabody, an employee of the New York World's Fair, has disappeared. Since the fair began on April 30, Pervious has had a perfect record for weight guessing. He never once gave out a Kewpie doll. Bystanders reported that Pervious became perturbed when one sly girl outwitted him.

An employee told police, 'Pervious was really upset over being tricked. He slammed things around, jumped up and down on the scale, and threw a bunch of Kewpie dolls in the fish pond.' Police questioned others nearby. Pervious's whereabouts remain a mystery."

A chill ran down Malcolm's back as he turned to Dandy.

"That sly girl was Grandma Eunice," he announced.

Ecto-Eyed!

Plop! Plop! Plop!

Malcolm and Dandy glanced at the bottle. It was tipped on its side again, dripping ectoplasm everywhere.

Malcolm quickly snatched it up. "Stop! You're getting ecto all over my Hello, UFO Alien Radar!"

It was the newest gadget he'd ordered from *Worlds Beyond* magazine. The radar looked like a skinny blue funnel glued on

top of an orange calculator. Malcolm had typed in 0.7734, then turned the calculator upside down so it said hELLO – a greeting to any extraterrestrial visitors. So far no aliens had said hello back, but if Pervious kept dripping ecto on his alien detector, Malcolm would never make contact.

"Pervious!" Malcolm called into the bottle. "We know you're in there. And you're going to have to come out."

Nothing.

Dandy picked up the bottle and put his eye to the opening. "I don't think he wants to come out."

Pervious answered by squirting a geyser of ecto right into Dandy's eye. "Yow!" Dandy shot back and danced around, wiping his eye with his fist. "He ecto-eyed me!"

"That does it," Malcolm said. He turned the bottle upside down and shook, hitting the bottom of it with the heel of his hand. "Come out of there!" But all that came out were a few drops of ecto that plopped to the floor.

"He's been in there so long, he probably has his own zip code," Dandy said, his eyelid nearly glued shut from the goop. "I don't think he's going to move out."

"He has to," Malcolm said, now banging the bottom of the bottle with his fist.

"If he doesn't," Dandy said, "we might drown in ectoplasm. You'll have to bury it again."

"Oh no, I won't. I like this bottle, and I plan to keep it. Without a ghost inside!" he yelled into it.

"So what do you plan to do?" Dandy asked.

"What I always do with pesky ghosts." He pulled out his Ecto-Handheld-Automatic-Heat-Sensitive-Laser-Enhanced Ghost Zapper and placed the nozzle to the opening in the bottle.

"It won't fit inside," Dandy pointed out.

"That's okay. Some of the zapper goo will get in." Malcolm squeezed the trigger.

Thick purple foam oozed up, drooled over the side, and covered the entire bottle.

"You have nowhere to run!" Malcolm shouted. He pulled the zapper away, stuck his thumb in the opening, and jiggled it at milkshake speed.

"This'll get you," he threatened. After a full minute, Malcolm removed his thumb.

"Do you think he's gone?" Dandy asked.

"Of course. No ghost can escape my zapper." He washed off the remaining zapper goo and smiled. "All done."

Dandy knitted his eyebrows. "Are you sure?" He leaned over and peeked into the top of the bottle. *Whoosh!* Another geyser of ecto splatted him in the eye. "Ahhhh!" He danced around again. "Ecto-eyed! Ecto-eyed!"

Malcolm held up the bottle. "That's impossible. He can't be in there."

"He's in there all right," Dandy said, his eye swollen shut. "And if you don't get rid of him, I might go blind."

Malcolm sneered. "He's hiding under the ectoplasm."

Dandy blinked. "And boy, he can make a lot of it."

Malcolm picked up his ghost detector. "You can hide from my zapper," he said to Pervious, "but you can't hide from my hound." He quickly flipped the power switch.

Go Away

Spooky materialized, snarling, growling, and baring his teeth.

Grrrr . . .

"Hear that, Pervious?" Malcolm said. "That's my dog. And he's not too happy you're here."

A small, twangy voice echoed up from the bottle. "Go away."

"Wow," Dandy said, "either he has severe allergies or he's holding his nose.

It sounds like he can't breathe."

Malcolm tilted his head toward Dandy. "Ghosts don't breathe, silly."

"I guess not," Dandy agreed, "but he sounds like he's got a snoot full of cotton balls."

"Oh great," Pervious whined. "First you try to kick me out of my house, and now you're making fun of me?"

"Sorry," Dandy apologized. "But you sure sound awfully stuffy for someone who likes to spit ecto in people's eyes."

"You don't sound very friendly," Pervious snipped. "You want to feed me to your dog."

Malcolm tried to reason with him. "It doesn't have to be this way. You can't stay in there. Your ecto is making a mess."

"I'm not leaving. This is my bottle. Mine!"

"No, it's not," Malcolm argued. "You gave it to my Grandma Eunice, then she gave it to me. It belongs to me."

Spooky was in a frenzy, yipping, yapping, and trying to get at the bottle.

"I don't see your name on it," Pervious taunted.

"I don't see your name on it either," Malcolm countered.

"It's written on the inside."

"Where?" Dandy asked, getting a little too close. *Splurt!* He caught another eyeful of ecto. "Ahhhh! Stop doing that!"

"That's it," Malcolm warned him. "I'm siccing my dog on you." He laid the bottle on the floor. "Get him, Spooky!"

Yip! Yip! Spooky sniffed, hopped over, sniffed again, then *whoosh!* disappeared inside.

The boys watched and waited. Seconds ticked by. Dandy looked at Malcolm. "Is he coming back out?"

Malcolm jiggled the bottle. "Spooky?"

Nothing.

"Now you have two ghosts in that bottle," Dandy pointed out.

But suddenly the bottle rumbled. It quivered and quaked. Malcolm set it back on the floor.

"Uh . . . Malcolm," Dandy started, his eyes wide, "I don't like this one bit."

"Don't worry," Malcolm said with a grin. "Spooky is tearing into him. I bet he's ripping a hole right in the seat of Pervious's pants."

The bottle continued to tremble. Harder and harder and harder . . . then . . . *Whack!*

Spooky came sailing out, covered in green guck.

"And stay out!" Pervious yelled.

Spooky whimpered and trotted to the far corner, his tail between his legs.

Malcolm narrowed his eyes. Anger welled up inside him. If he were any madder, smoke would come out of his ears. "You did not just kick my dog!"

"Yep, I did," Pervious said. "And I'll kick out anything else you send in here." And to make his point, he shot up a geyser of ecto that exploded into the air.

Dandy dodged, but not quick enough. Some of the green slime squirted his eye. The rest showered down, covering his Pump and Dunks. When he tried lifting his foot, strings of it stretched up like gum.

Pervious snorted laughter. "Boo-hoo. Is your daddy going to kill you?"

"Malcolm," Dandy said, "maybe we should just smash the bottle into itty pieces. He'd have to come out then."

Sure, breaking the bottle would leave Pervious homeless, but Malcolm intended to keep it . . . without Pervious inside.

"I've got a better idea," Malcolm whispered to Dandy. He stuck the cork back in the bottle and set it on the counter.

A Standoff

Dandy got his shoes unstuck from the ectoplasm and followed Malcolm upstairs. "Slow down," he said. "I can only see out of one eye."

But Malcolm was in a hurry. He intended to get Pervious out of that bottle one way or another. They got busy going from room to room.

First, they snuck into Cocoa's bedroom. Malcolm nabbed a spritzer of Non-Scents cologne, a pump bottle of Tiger Lily facial

lotion, and a V-shaped jar of zit cream.

Next they moved to Grandma Eunice's room. Malcolm found a flowery can of foot powder, a blue bottle of wart remover, and a rosy jar of anti-aging cream.

But the best finds were in the last room—the kitchen. Malcolm took down the Mrs. Butterworth's syrup, a teddy bear honey bottle, and a jam jar shaped like a cluster of grapes.

"This should do it," he said. The boys rushed back down to the basement.

Spooky cowered in the corner. He'd gotten so close to the wall, his tail had vanished into the drywall.

"Don't worry, Spooky," Malcolm said. "This will all be over soon."

"But how are we going to get all that ecto off of him?" Dandy asked.

"Good question," Malcolm answered. "But one problem at a time."

Malcolm carefully placed the bottles on the counter.

"Hey, Pervious," Malcolm sing-songed as he uncorked the World's Fair bottle. "I did some house hunting for you. It's time for an upgrade."

Pervious was suspiciously quiet.

"Aren't these bottles so much better than the one you're hiding in?" Malcolm said.

Still no sound from Pervious.

Malcolm set the World's Fair bottle down in the small village of containers he'd collected. "So much nicer."

He spritzed some of the Non-Scents cologne into the air. "Doesn't that smell wonderful?"

Pervious sneezed. So did Dandy. Malcolm took the cologne away. He pushed the wart remover forward. "I bet blue is your favorite color."

"My favorite color is gray," Pervious twanged.

Malcolm tilted his head. "Impossible. Nobody's favorite color is gray."

"Mine is," Pervious squeaked.

Dandy scratched his head. "I like gray."

"Shhh," Malcolm warned. "You're not helping."

Dandy shrugged and blinked, his green eyelid sticking shut. "Well, I do."

"Look at this one," Malcolm said to Pervious. He nudged the honey bottle forward. "It is a cute and cuddly bear."

"Are you trying to kill me?" Pervious spit. "I'm allergic to honey!"

"I can't kill you," Malcolm pointed out. "You're already dead."

"Oh yeah." Some ectoplasm oozed up and gurgled over the side of the bottle in Malcolm's hand.

"Try Mrs. Butterworth," Dandy whispered. "No one can resist her."

Malcolm scooted her forward. "Pervious, take a look at this one. I bet she looks just like your old granny. Aren't you homesick for her fresh baked cookies and sweet smile?"

"She reminds me of my third grade teacher, Mrs. Hogg," Pervious complained. "She used to make me stay after school and write, *I will not pull Peggy Potter's pigtails* a hundred times. I couldn't wait to get to fourth grade!"

Pervious shot a stream of ecto into the air. Dandy ducked under a table. Malcolm stamped a foot and crossed his arms. "Don't you like any of these bottles?"

"Yeah," Pervious answered. "Mine!" With that, he blew a raspberry. *Plllluurrrr!*

"Ahhhhh! That's it! I'm going to find a way to flush you out of there. And no amount of ectoplasm can hide you," Malcolm announced.

Blast Him Out

Malcolm thought about what he'd just said. *I'm going to find a way to flush you out of there.* He snatched up the bottle, completely covered in green goo, and rushed to the sink. He turned on the faucet full force and set the bottle underneath.

"Take that!" Within seconds the water inside shot up from the top.

"Think that'll wash him out?" Dandy asked.

Malcolm nodded. "Yep. And to make it worse, that water is scalding hot."

A minute passed. Lots of watered-down ecto spilled up and over, but no Pervious.

They waited another minute. Nothing. But then . . .

"Rub-a-dub-dub. Rub-a-dub-dub."

Dandy dared to move closer, putting his ear close. "Malcolm, I think he's singing."

"Pervious!" Malcolm shouted. "What are you doing in there?"

"Rub-a-dub-dub. Thanks, boys!" Pervious gargled up. "This is the first shower I've had in over seventy years!"

"Gah!" Malcolm stamped his foot again. He shut off the faucet and dumped out all the water. A string of ecto, gooier than Mrs. Butterworth's syrup, slipped out too.

Malcolm ran to the closet and pulled out the handheld Dust Scooper. He'd used it once as a ghost scooper. Now he'd use it on Pervious.

"Try to get out of this!" Placing the Dust Scooper over the bottle, he switched it on. *Vrrrrrrrm.*

Again, they waited.

But after about thirty seconds, the scooper sputtered and choked. *Wheeze . . . hut . . . wheeze . . . hut . . . wheeze.* It sounded just like Grandma Eunice when she had the hiccups.

"What's going on?" Dandy asked.

"I don't know." When Malcolm turned the scooper around to check—*splurrrrrt!*—a geyser of ecto shot out, soaking him and Dandy both from head to foot.

"Ahhhh!" They hopped around, wiping the goop from their eyes.

"Phew!" Pervious called from inside the bottle. "It seemed awfully windy for a bit."

Malcolm felt the blood rising to his face. "I'm going to get you, Pervious! You won't be in that bottle for long."

"Ooh, I'm so scared," Pervious taunted.

If Malcolm hadn't wanted that bottle so badly, he would've smashed it right then and there. "You wait. I *will* find a way to flush you out of there!"

A volcano of ecto gurgled over the side.

"Come on," Malcolm said to Dandy. "We need to regroup."

They went upstairs to clean up.

"Wow," Dandy said, looking in the bathroom mirror. "We look like walking asparagus."

Malcolm gritted his teeth. "Yeah. And I don't like it one bit."

Dandy grabbed the soap. It slipped from his fingers a few times, but he finally managed to hang on. "Maybe you should just bury the bottle again."

"Never."

"But your whole house will eventually look like this." Dandy pointed to his alien-green face and swollen eye.

"Not if I get Pervious out of there first," Malcolm said.

Dandy shook his head. "I don't know how. It's not like you can blast him out."

Suddenly, a light went on in Malcolm's brain. "Dandy, you're a genius!"

Dandy blinked a few times, his green eye sticking. "Huh?"

"That's what we'll do. We'll blast him out."

Dandy gaped like he'd just found out there'd be a pop quiz. "How will we do that?"

Malcolm grinned. "You'll see."

A Fair Ending

Once the boys were cleaned up, they went looking for Grandma Eunice. She was back in her bedroom, snacking on pretzels and watching a game show.

"Grandma," Malcolm asked sweetly, "do you have any of those large breath mints?"

Grandma Eunice cupped her hand to her mouth and said, "Does my breath stink? 'Cause I've got to keep it sweet and kissable."

Grandma's breath was a little sour, but Malcolm wasn't concerned about that.

"It's for us," Malcolm said to her.

She winked. "So you want to keep your breath kissable, too."

"Ew, no!" Malcolm shuddered. "We just need as many breath mints as you can spare," Malcolm said. "Pleeeeease?"

Grandma opened the drawer to her nightstand. It was filled with rolls and rolls of breath mints! She scooped up a big pile and handed them to Malcolm. "This will keep you kissable. The girls will be lining up."

"Ew!" Malcolm said again. But he didn't have time to be grossed out. "Thanks!" he called as he and Dandy rushed out.

Then they went into the kitchen. Malcolm grabbed a bottle of diet cola from

the fridge. "This will do it." He handed everything over to Dandy. "Take these outside. I'll be right there."

Malcolm hurried into the basement and snatched up his ghost detector and the World's Fair bottle.

"Wait. Where are you taking me?" Pervious demanded.

Malcolm smiled. "Out for some fresh air."

Once they were outside, Malcolm warned Dandy. "Stand back."

Dandy didn't argue. He moved way back. Then, Malcolm dropped the breath mints into the bottle.

Pervious sighed. "Mmmmm . . . minty."

"Not for long," Malcolm assured him. Then he turned to Dandy. "Time to have a blast."

Malcolm set the bottle down, poured in the soda, then jumped back. A few seconds later, *Whoosh!* A geyser of foamy cola shot up into the air and jetted over the fence, taking Pervious with it. *"Ahhhhhh!"* he bellowed, riding on a wave of cola.

Malcolm shook out the rest of the soda and quickly plugged the opening with his thumb. "He's gone!"

Dandy just stood, his mouth agape. "You made a missile out of diet soda and breath mints?"

Malcolm nodded. "Yep. A chemical bottle rocket."

Dandy beamed. "Cool!"

"Let's go," Malcolm said.

They rushed back down to the basement. Malcolm quickly cleaned out his ghost-free bottle and corked it.

Dandy tugged on Malcolm's sleeve. "Why is Spooky still spooked?"

The whimpering little pup still cowered in the corner.

Malcolm walked over. "What's wrong, boy?"

Then he heard a familiar voice coming from the table. "You tricked me!"

Malcolm whipped around. "Pervious?"

"He's in here," Dandy said, picking up Grandma Eunice's wart cream bottle.

"How dare you," Pervious scowled. "Get me out! Get me out! It smells like fried onions in here."

"I've got a better idea," Malcolm said. "Come on, Dandy. It's time to remove this wart."

They carried Pervious's new home outside and buried it under the flower bed.

Malcolm dusted off his hands. "He'll learn to like it."

When they got back to the basement, Spooky was bouncing and bounding. *Yip! Yip!*

Malcolm rolled a ball toward him to play. "Good boy."

After a few minutes, Dandy asked, "Don't you feel a little bit bad about sending Pervious away?"

He shook his head. "Are you kidding? The guy squirted us with ecto, nearly blinded you, and blew raspberries at us." Using both hands, Malcolm covered the words *World's* and *1939* on the bottle. "What we did was absolutely . . . fair!"

TOOLS OF THE TRADE: FIVE TOOLS FOR THE GHOST HUNTER ON THE GO

From Ghost Detectors Malcolm and Dandy

Sometimes, ghost detectors need to know how to speak the languages of different ghosts! Here are four phrases that would have come in handy for Malcolm and Dandy.

1. Kewpie doll - a brightly colored doll given as a prize at a carnival.

2. ruined - having a reputation that is damaged without possibility of repair.

3. weights - a game at a carnival where the person guesses how much you weigh.

4. 1939 World's Fair - a large, international exhibit of industrial, scientific, and cultural items. The 1939 World's Fair was held in New York City, New York.

Harris County Public Library
Houston, Texas